HOPSCOTCH
TWISTY TALES

Little Red Hen's Great Escape

by Elizabeth Dale

and Andrew Painter

W
FRANKLIN WATTS
LONDON•SYDNEY

This story is based on the traditional fairy tale,
The Little Red Hen, but with a new twist.
You can read the original story in
Must Know Stories. Can you make
up your own twist for the story?

Franklin Watts
First published in Great Britain in 2015 by The Watts Publishing Group

ISBN 978 1 4451 4304 0 (hbk)
ISBN 978 1 4451 4305 7 (pbk)
ISBN 978 1 4451 4307 1 (library ebook)

Series Editor: Melanie Palmer
Series Advisor: Catherine Glavina
Series Designer: Peter Scoulding
Cover Designer: Cathryn Gilbert

Printed in China

Franklin Watts
An imprint of
Hachette Children's Group
Part of The Watts Publishing Group
Carmelite House
50 Victoria Embankment
London EC4Y 0DZ

An Hachette UK Company
www.hachette.co.uk

www.franklinwatts.co.uk

The Little Red Hen was worried.
Bulldozers had arrived in the
farmyard. Holes were being dug.
Something bad was going on.

3

She went to see Farmer Green.
She knew he wouldn't tell her
what was happening, so she had
to be clever.

"The builders are so busy,"
she clucked. "Can I help?"
"You!" laughed the farmer.
"How can you help?"

5

"I can pick up sand and straw to keep everywhere tidy," the Little Red Hen said.

"OK," said the farmer.
"Be helpful while you can."
The Little Red Hen trembled
with fear. What did he mean?

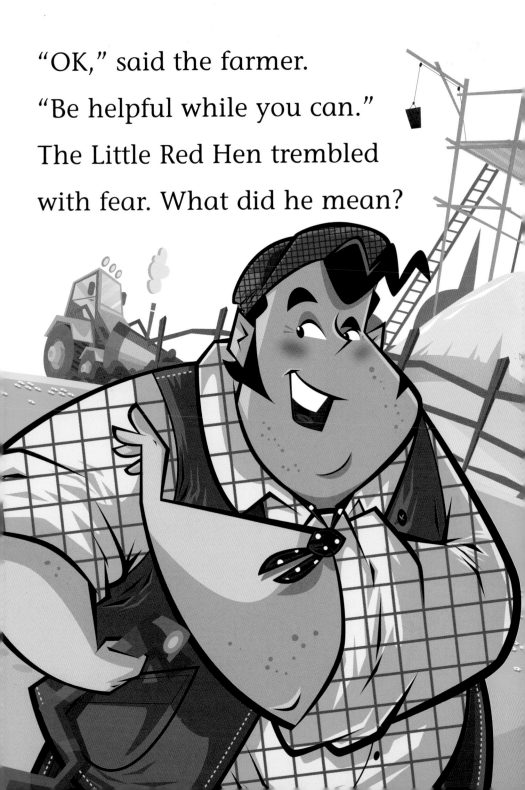

"Something terrible is happening," she told the pig, the lamb and the duck. "Please help me to find out what it is!"

"Not until eleven o'cluck!"

snorted the pig.

"No thank ewe,"

laughed the lamb.

"You're just chicken!"
quacked the duck.

"Lazy animals!" thought the
Little Red Hen.

"Something terrible's happening," she told the chickens. "Please help me find out what."

"What are you, the little Head Hen?" clucked one.

"No," said the Little Red Hen.

"But we're in danger. No one else will help."

The poor Little Red Hen looked
so worried.

"OK!" said the chickens.

"Brilliant!" clucked the Little Red Hen. "Keep your beaks to the ground, your eyes wide open and report back."

So the chickens scurried all over
the farmyard, beaks to the ground,
eyes wide open. So did the chicks.

16

Some chickens picked up sand, while some pecked through a big cloth. Others flew around the farm, while the Little Red Hen read the plans.

They all met back in the barn.

"There are piles of bricks!" clucked one chick.

"Steel doors!" said another.

"Big walls!" said a third.

"They're planning to keep every animal cooped up inside!" cried the Little Red Hen. "We must tell the others!"

"You need some oinkment!" snorted the pig.

"You're utterly quackers!" quacked the duck.

"You're baaa–king maaaad!"
bleated the lamb.

"Well, all the chickens are
leaving!" said the Little Red Hen.
And they did.

The next day, the farmer came
to fetch all the animals.
"Come for a lovely walk,"
he told them.

"Isn't he nice," said the pig, the lamb and the duck. "The Little Red Hen was just being silly!"

23

"In you come," smiled the farmer, opening up a door.

"Help!" cried the pig, the lamb and the duck.

The chickens pushed the farmer inside! Clunk! went the door. Click! went the key.

"Hooray!" cried the pig, the lamb and the duck, making faces at the farmer.

27

To celebrate their escape, the
animals had a brilliant party.

"Please help clean up!" said the Little Red Hen. So the animals did – after all, they'd learned their lesson.

Puzzle 1

Put these pictures in the correct order.
Which event do you think is most important?
Now try writing the story in your own words!

Puzzle 2

1. I have got a surprise for the animals!

2. I have found a secret plan.

3. We work well as a team.

4. There is lots of work to do.

5. We have been spying.

6. Something isn't right on the farm.

Choose the correct speech bubbles for each character. Can you think of any others? Turn over to find the answers.

Answers

Puzzle 1

The correct order is: 1c, 2f, 3e, 4a, 5b, 6d

Puzzle 2

The Little Red Hen: 2, 6

The farmer: 1, 4

The chicks: 3, 5

Look out for more Hopscotch Twisty Tales and Must Know Stories:

TWISTY TALES

The Lovely Duckling
ISBN 978 1 4451 1633 4

Hansel and Gretel and the Green Witch
ISBN 978 1 4451 1634 1

The Emperor's New Kit
ISBN 978 1 4451 1635 8

Rapunzel and the Prince of Pop
ISBN 978 1 4451 1636 5

Dick Whittington Gets on his Bike
ISBN 978 1 4451 1637 2

The Pied Piper and the Wrong Song
ISBN 978 1 4451 1638 9

The Princess and the Frozen Peas
ISBN 978 1 4451 0675 5

Snow White Sees the Light
ISBN 978 1 4451 0676 2

The Elves and the Trendy Shoes
ISBN 978 1 4451 0678 6

The Three Frilly Goats Fluff
ISBN 978 1 4451 0677 9

Princess Frog
ISBN 978 1 4451 0679 3

Rumpled Stilton Skin
ISBN 978 1 4451 0680 9

Jack and the Bean Pie
ISBN 978 1 4451 0182 8

Brownilocks and the Three Bowls of Cornflakes
ISBN 978 1 4451 0183 5

Cinderella's Big Foot
ISBN 978 1 4451 0184 2

Little Bad Riding Hood
ISBN 978 1 4451 0185 9

Sleeping Beauty – 100 Years Later
ISBN 978 1 4451 0186 6

**MUST KNOW STORIES
LEVEL1:**
The Gingerbread Man
ISBN 978 1 4451 2819 1*
ISBN 978 1 4451 2820 7

The Three Little Pigs
ISBN 978 14451 2823 8*
ISBN 978 14451 2824 5

Jack and the Beanstalk
ISBN 978 14451 2827 6*
ISBN 978 14451 2828 3

The Boy Who Cried Wolf
ISBN 978 14451 2831 3*
ISBN 978 14451 2832 0

The Three Billy Goats Gruff
ISBN 978 14451 2835 1*
ISBN 978 14451 2836 8

The Three Billy Goats Gruff
ISBN 978 14451 2835 1*
ISBN 978 14451 2836 8

Little Red Riding Hood
ISBN 978 14451 2839 9*
ISBN 978 14451 2840 5

Goldilocks and the Three Bears
ISBN 978 14451 2843 6 *
ISBN 978 14451 2844 3

Hansel and Gretel
ISBN 978 14451 2847 4*
ISBN 978 14451 2848 1

The Little Red Hen
ISBN 978 14451 2851 1*
ISBN 978 14451 2852 8

Dick Whittington
ISBN 978 14451 2855 9*
ISBN 978 14451 2856 6

Rapunzel
ISBN 978 14451 2859 7*
ISBN 978 14451 2860 3